TO LEWIS AND STRUAN,
TWO LITTLE BOYS WHO GREW UP
AND FOUND THEIR BIG-BOY VOICES.

THIS BOOK IS GIVEN WITH LOVE

TO:

_____

FROM:

_____

COCK-A DOODLE

DON'T YOU DARE!

WRITTEN BY: IAN MCARTHUR   ILLUSTRATED BY: EDUARDO PAJ

ROBBIE WAS A ROOSTER,
WHO FOUND IT HARD TO CROW.
BUT WHY HE MADE SUCH AWFUL SOUNDS,
HE REALLY DID NOT KNOW.

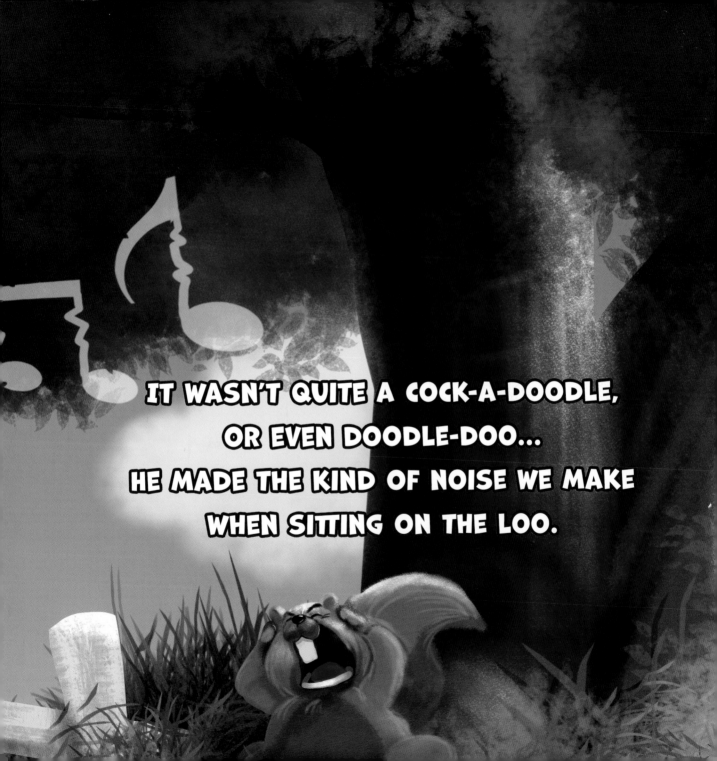

IT WASN'T QUITE A COCK-A-DOODLE,
OR EVEN DOODLE-DOO...
HE MADE THE KIND OF NOISE WE MAKE
WHEN SITTING ON THE LOO.

THE PORKY PIGS DID TAUNT AND SCOFF,
THEY'D ROLL THEIR EYES AND GLARE,
BEFORE ROBBIE GOT THE CHANCE TO CROW,
THEY'D OINK,"COCK-A-DOODLE...

DON'T YOU DARE!"

THE WOOLLY SHEEP LAUGHED AND MOCKED,
THEY REALLY WERE NOT FAIR.
BEFORE ROBBIE GOT A CHANCE TO CROW,
THEY'D BAA, "COCK-A-DOODLE...

DON'T YOU DARE!"

THE COWS WOULD ALL MAKE FUN OF HIM,
FOR HIS SOUND WAS HARD TO BEAR.
BEFORE ROBBIE GOT THE CHANCE TO CROW,
THEY'D MOO, "COCK-A-DOODLE...

DON'T YOU DARE!"

"WHY CAN'T I COCK-A-DOODLE-DOO?"
ROBBIE WONDERED WHY.
WHEN HE COULDN'T FIND THE ANSWER,
A TEAR DROPPED FROM HIS EYE.

HE WENT TO SEE HIS FRIEND STEVE,
A SWAN WHO LIVED ON THE FARM,
TO TELL HIM ABOUT THIS PROBLEM,
FOR SURELY IT WOULDN'T DO HARM!

SO, HE HAD A TALK WITH STEVE THE SWAN,
WHO WAS ONCE AN UGLY DUCK.
HE LISTENED TO WHAT ROBBIE SAID,
AND WHAT A STROKE OF LUCK!

STEVE THE SWAN WAS OLD AND WISE,
AND HAD HELPED IN MANY A CRISIS.
HE KNEW WHY ROBBIE COULDN'T CROW...
HE HAD
"COCK-A-DOODLE-ITUS!"

"COCK-A-DOODLE-ITUS" IS A NASTY THING,
A PROBLEM BOTH MEAN AND CRUEL.
IT HAPPENS WHEN OTHERS MAKE FUN OF YOU,
AND THEY TAKE YOU FOR A FOOL.

"NO ONE ELSE IS QUITE LIKE YOU,
YOU REALLY ARE UNIQUE.
JUST LOVE WHAT MAKES YOU DIFFERENT,
EVEN THAT SOUND FROM YOUR BEAUTIFUL BEAK."

THIS MADE ROBBIE FEEL GOOD INSIDE,
TO CROW LOUDLY WAS NOW HIS DESIRE.
BUT SUDDENLY HE SMELT SOMETHING STRANGE,
IT WAS SMOKE FROM A RAGING FIRE!

"OH NO!" CRIED ROBBIE.
"WHAT SHALL WE DO, WHATEVER IS GOING ON?"
THE SMELL WAS GETTING STRONGER NOW,
A REALLY SMOKEY PONG!

NOW IN THE DARK, THE ANIMALS
WERE SNORING ON THE FARM.
SO, WHAT COULD ROBBIE AND STEVE DO,
TO QUICKLY RAISE AN ALARM?

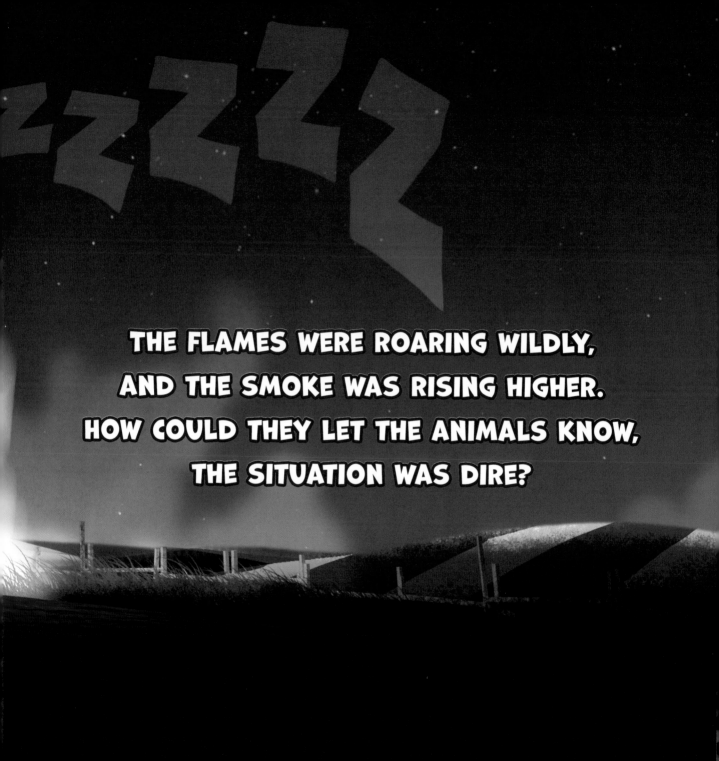

THE FLAMES WERE ROARING WILDLY,
AND THE SMOKE WAS RISING HIGHER.
HOW COULD THEY LET THE ANIMALS KNOW,
THE SITUATION WAS DIRE?

THEN OUT OF NOWHERE CAME A SOUND,
NEVER HEARD BEFORE.
A SOUND TO WAKE UP ALL THE LAND,
AND STOP EVERY SINGLE SNORE.

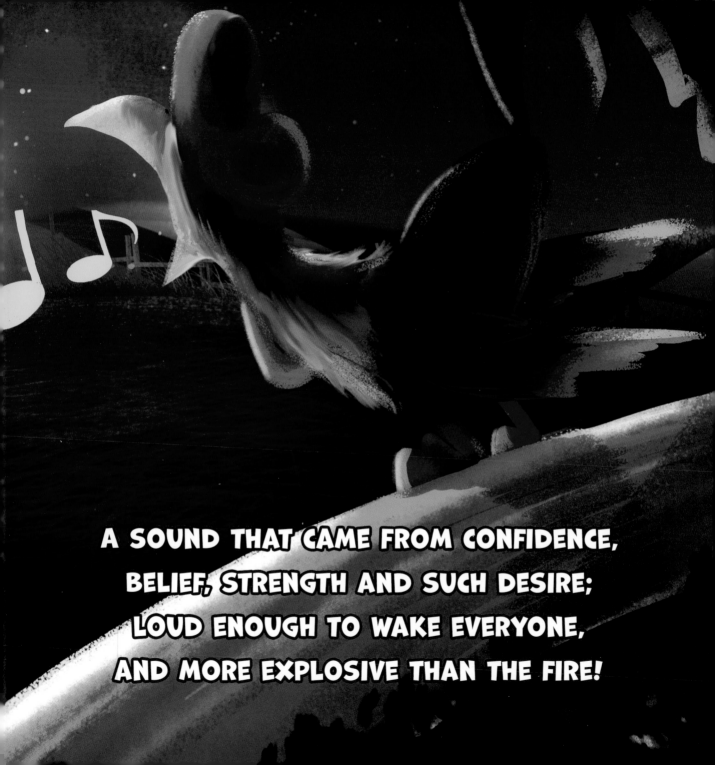

A SOUND THAT CAME FROM CONFIDENCE,
BELIEF, STRENGTH AND SUCH DESIRE;
LOUD ENOUGH TO WAKE EVERYONE,
AND MORE EXPLOSIVE THAN THE FIRE!

THE ANIMALS STOPPED THEIR SNORING,
WOKEN UP BY A
"COCK-A-DOODLE-DOO!"
THEY RUSHED OUTSIDE AND SAW THE FLAMES,
ASKING, "WHO MADE THAT NOISE, JUST WHO?"

THEN SUDDENLY, THE ANSWER DAWNED,
FOR EVERY ANIMAL ON THE FARM.
THEY KNEW WHO'D SAVED THEM FROM THE FIRE,
AND WHO HAD BRAVELY RAISED THE ALARM.

IT WAS SOMEONE THEY HAD MOCKED AND SHAMED,
WITH THEIR OINKS AND BAAS AND MOOS.
BUT NOW THEY THANKED THEIR LUCKY STARS
FOR ROBBIE'S

COCK-A-DOODLE-DOO!

FROM THAT DAY ON THE ANIMALS WOULD SMILE,
AND SING AS HE CAME INTO VIEW.
AND ROBBIE WOULD JOIN IN THE CHORUS WITH PRIDE,

"COCK-A-DOODLE-DOO!"

WITH HIS SPECIAL

CLAIM YOUR FREE GIFT!

VISIT:

 **PDICBOOKS.COM/GIFT**

THANK YOU FOR PURCHASING

COCK-A-DOODLE DON'T YOU DARE!

AND WELCOME TO THE PUPPY DOGS & ICE CREAM FAMILY.

WE'RE CERTAIN YOU'RE GOING TO LOVE THE LITTLE GIFT

WE'VE PREPARED FOR YOU AT THE WEBSITE ABOVE.